Alexandre Dumas
was born in 1802. The son of a famous Napoleonic
general, Dumas loved adventure and history. *The Three
Musketeers*, *The Count of Monte Cristo* and *The Man in
the Iron Mask* feature both. He died in 1870.

French Pronunciation Key
These French words are in **bold** the first time they appear.

Stress the syllable in capital letters.

Amiens: a-me-AN

Aramis: a-ra-MIS

Athos: at-TOES

Bonacieux: bone-a-see-UH

Calais: cal-LAY

Cardinal: car-dee-NAL

Comte: cont

Constance: con-stans

d'Artangan: dar-tan-NYON

de Rochefort: duh rosh-FOR

de Tréville: duh tray-VEEL

en garde: on gard

Hôtel de Ville: oh-TELL duh vee

Louis: loo-WEE

Meung: mun

Monsieur: miss-YUH

Porthos: por-TOES

Richelieu: rish-uh-LUH

Cover illustration by Mike Jaroszko

Copyright © Ladybird Books USA 1996

Originally published in the United Kingdom by
Ladybird Books Ltd © 1994

First American edition by Ladybird Books USA
An Imprint of Penguin USA Inc.
375 Hudson Street, New York, New York 10014

Printed in Great Britain

10 9 8 7 6 5 4 3 2 1

ISBN 0-7214-5610-3

Ladybird

PICTURE CLASSICS

THE THREE MUSKETEERS

by Alexandre Dumas

Retold by Leslie Kimmelman
Illustrated by David Barnett
Woodcuts by Jonathan Mercer

A crowd gathered outside the town's inn

D'ARTAGNAN

On the first Monday in April, 1625, the little French town of **Meung** was in a great state of excitement. Fighting was common in those times. France fought Spain, nobleman fought nobleman, and the King fought with the powerful **Cardinal Richelieu**. Few days passed without the clashing of swords or the firing of muskets.

On this day, a noisy and curious crowd gathered outside the town's inn. A young man had just arrived, riding an old, oddly-colored horse. The yellow animal, with its dragging head, was so funny-looking that many of the townspeople could hardly keep from laughing. But the long, sharp sword at the stranger's side and the proud gleam in his eye convinced them to be quiet.

The young man's name was **d'Artagnan**. He was on his way to the city of Paris, where he hoped to fulfill his greatest wish — to become a King's Musketeer. He was carrying a letter of introduction to **Monsieur de Tréville**, the captain of the Musketeers and an old friend of his father's.

As he dismounted from his horse, d'Artagnan saw a man with a scar on his forehead standing at the inn's window, talking to friends and laughing loudly. Clearly, it was d'Artagnan and his horse that they found so funny.

"Are you laughing at me?" challenged d'Artagnan, drawing his sword.

"I laugh when it pleases me," the man replied.

"And I," cried d'Artagnan, "only allow people to laugh when it pleases me!" He lunged with his sword. The man with the scar drew his sword, too. But the innkeeper and several onlookers, anxious to prevent a fight, hit d'Artagnan with sticks and shovels. They knocked him to the ground and stopped the duel before it began. Then they carried d'Artagnan inside to have his wounds tended to.

When the innkeeper returned, the man with the scar asked, "How and who is that young man?"

"He will soon be good as new, your Excellency," answered the innkeeper. "I don't know who he is, sir, but he has with him a letter to M. de Tréville in Paris."

"Really!" replied the man with the scar. "I wonder what is in that letter."

"The letter is in his vest pocket, which is in the kitchen," the innkeeper told him. "The young man," he continued slyly, "is upstairs, being nursed by my wife."

"Get my bill ready and my horse saddled," ordered the man, heading toward the kitchen. He added to himself, "I must hurry to meet Milady and then leave at once."

Feeling a little better, d'Artagnan limped into the courtyard. The first thing he saw was the man with the scar, talking to a beautiful young woman in a carriage.

"What are the Cardinal's wishes?" he heard her ask.

"Return to England at once, Milady," the man with the scar replied. "Keep a close watch on the Duke of Buckingham, and let the Cardinal know as soon as he leaves London. I myself am going to Paris."

D'Artagnan didn't understand any of the conversation. But he rushed forward, sword in hand. "Stand and fight, sir!" he demanded. "That is, unless you dare run away in front of a lady."

Seeing her companion reach for his sword, Milady touched his arm. "Remember," she told him, "any delay could ruin our plans."

"You're right," he agreed. "Go your way and I'll go mine."

He galloped off in one direction, and the carriage moved in another, leaving d'Artagnan alone.

"Stand and fight, sir!"

"Coward!" he yelled after the man with the scar. "But she was a beautiful lady," he murmured to himself.

D'Artagnan was about to leave for Paris when he discovered that his letter was missing. "My letter!" he cried. "It's lost!"

"Perhaps stolen," said the innkeeper innocently. "The man with the scar must have taken it. He was very interested in that letter," the innkeeper added.

Now all d'Artagnan could do was hope that M. de Tréville would see him anyway.

AT MONSIEUR DE TRÉVILLE'S

In such dangerous times, King **Louis** XIII of France needed brave, loyal men at his side. M. de Tréville led the King's Musketeers, a band of courageous men sworn to protect the King.

Almost as powerful as the King was Cardinal Richelieu, an ambitious and untrustworthy man. The Cardinal had his own company of Guards — bitter enemies of the King's Musketeers.

When d'Artagnan arrived at M. de Tréville's headquarters, his heart pounded with excitement. He was allowed to see M. de Tréville, but he had to wait while the captain of the Musketeers lectured three of his men.

"**Athos! Porthos! Aramis!**" the captain began

"They attacked us!" the Musketeers protested

angrily. "I am told that you were fighting in the streets yesterday and almost caused a riot. Then you were arrested by the Cardinal's Guards. Is this true?"

"They attacked us!" protested the three. "And we did not embarrass you. We fought back and escaped."

"This I did not know," said M. de Tréville. "But I will not let my men risk their lives for nothing. The King needs brave men, especially his Musketeers. Now go, and I will see this young stranger."

When the three Musketeers had left the room, d'Artagnan eagerly introduced himself. He told M. de Tréville about the stolen letter and explained that he had come to Paris to join the Musketeers.

"No one joins the Musketeers until he proves himself worthy with his sword," M. de Treville explained. "But because I liked your father, I will do my best to help you. I will send you to the Royal Academy, where you will learn horsemanship and the art of the sword."

"You won't be disappointed, I promise, sir," said d'Artagnan, bowing. "Thank you."

Just then, through the window, d'Artagnan spotted the man with the scar. In his rush to reach the man, d'Artagnan bumped, one by one, into Athos, Porthos, and Aramis. Still recovering from the scolding they had received, they were easily offended. D'Artagnan made each of them so mad, that each Musketeer challenged him to a duel — the first at noon, the second at one o'clock, and the last at two o'clock!

D'Artagnan shook his head. "I can't back out now," he said to himself. "But if I am killed, at least I will be killed by a Musketeer."

A SURPRISING DUEL

D'Artagnan didn't know anyone in Paris so he went to his first duel, with Athos, alone, but determined to fight his best. When Athos arrived, Porthos and Aramis were with him. They were astonished to discover that they had each separately made plans to fight the same young man.

"Now that you are all here," d'Artagnan said, "allow me to apologize."

The three Musketeers sneered, thinking d'Artagnan a coward.

D'Artagnan quickly set them straight. "You misunderstand me, gentlemen. I am not afraid. I apologize only in case I am killed before all three of you have had the chance to fight me. And now, Monsieur Athos, **en garde!**"

D'Artagnan drew his sword. Athos drew his just as a company of the Cardinal's Guards appeared.

"Put your swords away!" Porthos and Aramis called in warning, but it was too late.

"Fighting again, Musketeers?" taunted one of the Guards. "Dueling is against the law. I arrest you in the name of the Cardinal. Put down your swords."

"Never!" cried the three Musketeers. "There may be only three of us, but we will fight to the finish."

"You are wrong," said d'Artagnan quietly. "There are four of us, not three. I may not be a Musketeer yet, but I am one in spirit."

"What's your name, brave fellow?" asked Athos.

"D'Artagnan, Monsieur."

"Well, then, Athos, Porthos, Aramis, and d'Artagnan, forward!" cried Athos.

Swords clashed, and the men fought fiercely. The Guards were skilled swordsmen, but at last they were defeated.

Afterward the four men returned to Monsieur de

A company of the Cardinals guards appeared

Tréville's headquarters arm in arm. D'Artagnan had never felt prouder.

This incident caused quite a commotion in Paris. M. de Tréville scolded his Musketeers in public, but congratulated them in private for the courage they'd shown. The King was so impressed with what he heard of young d'Artagnan that he made him a cadet in one of his other companies of guards.

From then on, d'Artagnan and the three Musketeers were the best of friends. D'Artagnan looked forward to the day when he, too, would become a true Musketeer.

A DISAPPEARANCE

One day, d'Artagnan's landlord came to see him.

"I've heard you are a brave man, d'Artagnan," said **Bonacieux**, "and I need help. My wife, **Constance**, has been kidnapped!"

"Kidnapped?" d'Artagnan repeated, surprised.

"My wife is the Queen's seamstress," explained Bonacieux. "She is also her friend — one of the few people the Queen can trust."

D'Artagnan had heard much about Queen Anne. He knew that the King no longer loved her and left her alone most of the time. The Cardinal once cared for her, but she rejected him.

The Duke of Buckingham, a powerful man in England, was said to be in love with Queen Anne. But England and France were not on friendly terms,

D'Artagnan jumped up

and falling in love with a foreign queen was a dangerous thing.

Bonacieux sighed. "I think my wife was kidnapped so they could force her to tell the Queen's secrets. Constance told me that the Queen is frightened. She believes Cardinal Richelieu has set a trap for the Duke of Buckingham — sending a letter to him with the Queen's signature, inviting him to Paris."

"You think the Cardinal is behind your wife's kidnapping?" d'Artagnan asked.

"I fear so," replied Bonacieux. "One of his men was seen nearby just as she was being kidnapped. A man with a long scar on his forehead."

D'Artagnan jumped up. "The man from Meung!"

"Then you will help me?" Bonacieux begged. "Since you are always with the Musketeers, and they are the Cardinal's enemies, I thought you might be glad of a chance to spoil his plans and help Queen Anne. In return, I will forget the three months rent you owe me."

"I'll do what I can," d'Artagnan promised. "And if he is the man I think he is, I have a score of my own to settle with him."

D'Artagnan lost no time in telling Athos, Porthos, and Aramis of the disappearance of Constance Bonacieux.

"This woman is in trouble because of her loyalty," he told them. "And I fear for the Queen's safety, too."

"I've heard people say that she loves our enemies, the Spanish and the English, more than she loves her own countrymen," said Athos.

"Spain is her native country," d'Artagnan reminded him. "It's only natural that she should love the Spanish. As for the English, it is only one man she admires, not the entire country. The Cardinal is using her admiration for this man to hatch a wicked plot against her."

The four friends had no doubt that their true enemy was the Cardinal. If they could upset his plans, it would be worth any danger they might risk. Clearly, the kidnapping of Constance was the key to the whole plot.

With outstretched hands, the four men vowed solemnly, "All for one and one for all!"

A SECRET MEETING

D'Artagnan's job was to watch Bonacieux's apartment from the upper floor. Bonacieux had been arrested, and now the Cardinal's men were using his house as a trap. Anyone who arrived was taken away and questioned about the Queen.

Late one night, d'Artagnan heard a woman scream. He drew his sword and rushed downstairs to help. The woman was Constance Bonacieux! She had escaped and returned home, not knowing that the Cardinal's men were waiting there. Now they were trying to force her to talk.

D'Artagnan's attack surprised the Guards and they ran off, leaving Constance in his care.

"Thank you for saving me," she said. "But I cannot stay. There is something I must do

He drew his sword and rushed downstairs

something for the Queen." With that, Constance hurried out the door.

Several hours later d'Artagnan saw her walking along a dark street with a man in a Musketeer's uniform. What could they be up to? He hurried to them and discovered that the man was a stranger, disguised as a Musketeer.

The stranger was the Duke of Buckingham. Constance was taking him to the palace for a secret meeting with the Queen. "Please don't give us away," she begged d'Artagnan. "You could ruin us all!"

D'Artagnan shook the Duke's hand. "I will see that you arrive safely."

Once there, Madame Bonacieux led the Duke into a quiet room where he could speak privately to the Queen. Buckingham had come to Paris in response to a message. But the message had been a trap set by the Cardinal.

Even though the Duke knew he was in danger,

he refused to return to England until he was sure that Queen Anne was safe.

When the Queen arrived, her beautiful face was pale with worry. She begged the Duke to return to England and not to see her again in secret.

"Come back as an ambassador, surrounded by guards," she told him. "For only then will you be safe in France."

"I will go," the Duke finally agreed. "But first I must have something to remind me of you until we meet again."

Queen Anne went into another room and returned with a gold-trimmed jewelry box. "Here," she said, giving him the box. "Keep this in memory of me. Now go before it is too late!"

Then our plan has failed

THE CARDINAL'S PLAN

Cardinal Richelieu soon learned of the Queen's secret meeting with Buckingham. **Comte de Rochefort** — the man with the scar — brought him the news. He was a friend of the Cardinal's and had placed a spy in the Queen's own household.

"The Queen and Buckingham met briefly," he told the Cardinal. "He has already left for England."

"Then our plan has failed," said the Cardinal.

"The Queen gave him a gift," Rochefort continued. "It was a box containing twelve diamond studs that had been her birthday gift from the King."

"Well, well," said the Cardinal, smiling slyly. "All is not lost."

He sat down and wrote a letter. Closing it with his seal, he sent for a servant.

"Take this to London at once," he ordered. "Stop for no one."

The letter said:

Milady de Winter —
   Be at the first ball the Duke of Buckingham attends. He will be wearing twelve diamond studs. Cut off two, and when you have them, inform me at once.

Next, the Cardinal asked for an audience with the King. He told him all about Buckingham's meeting with the Queen. The King was furious. He demanded to know the reason for the meeting.

"No doubt to plot with your enemies," replied the Cardinal.

"Why would he come to see the Queen? They are in love with each other," insisted the King.

"No, no, I cannot believe it," said the Cardinal, pretending to be loyal to the Queen, but also wanting to make the King suspicious. He added, "Yet I am told she has been crying and writing letters all morning."

"I must have those letters!" cried the King. He immediately sent his men to search the Queen's rooms. But the only letter he found was one addressed to the Queen's brother. She was hurt and very angry at the attack on her honor.

Feeling remorseful, the King wondered out loud how he would earn her forgiveness. Now the Cardinal was ready to put his plan into action.

"Perhaps if you did something to please the Queen," he advised cunningly, "her heart would soften. Why not give a ball for her? You know how much she loves to dance, and it would give her a chance to wear those beautiful diamonds you gave her."

Queen Anne was surprised and happy to hear

31

about the ball, and she soon forgave her husband. She asked eagerly when it was to take place.

"Cardinal Richelieu is arranging everything," replied the King. But every day the Cardinal made excuses for not setting the date.

Finally, on the tenth day, the Cardinal received a note which said:

I have the diamond studs. Send money, and I will bring them to Paris.

The Cardinal knew that Milady could travel from London to Paris in twelve days. He went to see the King.

"Today is the twentieth of September," he said. "We will have the ball on the third of October in the **Hôtel de Ville**. Don't forget, Sire, to tell Her Majesty that you want her to wear the diamonds."

The Queen was delighted when she learned that the ball was to be so soon. But her delight turned

The Queen was delighted

to fear when the King said, "I would like you to dress in your most beautiful gown. And please wear the diamonds I gave you for your birthday."

Queen Anne went pale with shock. "The ball and the date, these were the Cardinal's idea?"

"Yes, Madame, but why do you ask?" replied the King.

"And wearing the diamonds, that was his idea, too?" asked the Queen.

"What does it matter if it was?" demanded the King. "Do I ask too much?"

"No, Sire," the Queen answered softly.

"Then you will appear as I ask?"

"Yes, Sire."

"Very well," said the King, leaving the room. "I will count on it."

The Queen sank into a chair. "I am lost," she said hopelessly. "The Cardinal must know everything. What am I to do? Who will help me?" She began to weep.

"Don't cry, your Majesty," said a sweet voice. It was Constance Bonancieux, who had overheard all that the King and Queen had said to each other. "Don't be afraid," she told the Queen. "I would do anything for you. And I promise we will get back your jewels in time for the ball."

I must go on a secret mission for the Queen

THE JOURNEY

Constance knew she couldn't trust her husband. Before releasing him from prison, Cardinal Richelieu had given him a lot of money. Now he was a spy for the Cardinal. The only man she could trust was d'Artagnan. Knowing he would never betray the Queen, she went to him and told him all that had happened.

"I will start for London at once," d'Artagnan promised.

D'Artagnan asked Monsieur de Tréville if he could arrange a leave of absence for him. "I must go to England," he explained. "On a secret mission for the Queen."

M. de Tréville looked at him sharply. "Will anyone try to stop you?"

"The Cardinal would, if he knew," admitted d'Artagnan.

"Then you must not go alone," said M. de Tréville. "On such a dangerous mission it's much better to have four men. Then surely one of you will get through."

"Thank you," said d'Artagnan gratefully. He quickly rounded up Athos, Porthos, and Aramis.

The four adventurers snuck out of Paris in the middle of the night. They rode quietly, expecting an attack at any minute. As the sun rose, they started to relax.

In Chantilly, they stopped at an inn for breakfast. After the meal came the first sign of danger. A stranger who had shared their table called upon Porthos to drink to the Cardinal's health. Porthos agreed, if the stranger would then drink to the health of the King. The stranger shouted that he'd drink to no one but the Cardinal, and a bitter argument followed. Leaving Porthos to settle it, the others hurried on their way. Porthos could catch up with them later.

They traveled for several more hours when they came upon a group of men repairing the road. As they neared, the workmen pulled out concealed weapons and began to fight.

"Ambush!" cried d'Artagnan. "Ride!"

They quickly urged their horses onward. They escaped, but Aramis was wounded in the shoulder and could not travel much further. Athos and d'Artagnan left him in a nearby village to be looked after.

Now only Athos and d'Artagnan were left. They suspected the attacks were the work of the Cardinal. They rode all day and stopped in the evening in **Amiens**. The night passed peacefully, but when Athos went to pay the bill in the morning, the landlord accused him of using counterfeit money. Four armed men, who had clearly been waiting, rushed in and attacked.

"Ride on, d'Artagnan!" shouted Athos, his sword drawn. "Hurry!"

D'Artagnan galloped on and finally reached **Calais**, on the coast of France. He ran to a ship ready to sail for England. A tired-looking man was asking the ship's captain to take him aboard. The captain explained that, by order of the Cardinal, no one could leave France without his express permission.

"I already have the Cardinal's permission," the man said, showing the captain a paper. "Will you take me?"

The captain insisted that the pass be signed by the port governor. Hearing this, d'Artagnan hurried away and waited for the man to come back with the signed pass.

D'Artagnan was determined to have the pass bearing the Cardinal's name for himself. At first he simply asked for the paper, but when the man refused, d'Artagnan fought fiercely and took it.

"Ride on, d'Artagnan!" shouted Athos

Finally, pass in hand and a fresh wound in his chest, d'Artagnan boarded the ship and headed for England.

THE QUEEN'S DIAMONDS

D'Artagnan's ship sailed out of the harbor just as a cannon boomed, signaling that the port was closed.

Worn out by his adventures, d'Artagnan bandaged his wound and fell fast asleep. In the morning he watched anxiously as the ship dropped anchor in Dover, on the coast of England. After several hours on horseback, d'Artagnan arrived in London.

The young Frenchman didn't know any English, but he had a piece of paper with Buckingham's name written on it. Everyone in London knew of the Duke, and d'Artagnan was soon shown the way to his house.

Buckingham remembered him from their meeting that dark night on the streets of Paris.

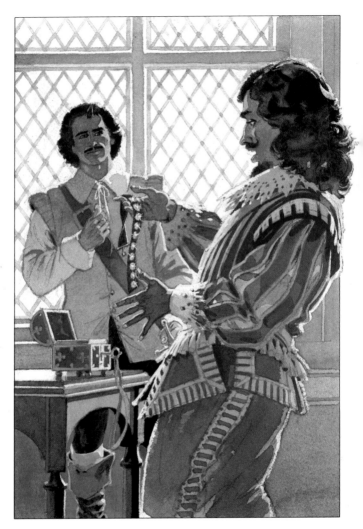

"Two of them are missing!"

When he was told of the danger Queen Anne was in, he was very concerned.

"I must return the diamonds to her at once!" he exclaimed. "Louis must never know she gave them to me." Taking a key from a chain he wore around his neck, the Duke unlocked the jewel box and lifted out the diamonds. Then he cried, "Two of them are missing!"

"Could you have lost them, my lord?" d'Artagnan wondered.

"Never!" the Duke said. "Look here — the ribbon that held them has been carefully cut. The diamonds were stolen!"

"But how?" asked d'Artagnan.

The Duke thought for a moment. "Wait!" he said suddenly. "I wore them only once, at a ball in London. Milady de Winter was there and she was especially friendly. I wondered why. She must have taken the diamonds at the request of the Cardinal. Oh, how could I have been so foolish?"

He paced up and down, thinking. The ball was in five days. If Queen Anne appeared with two of the diamonds missing, the King would be furious, and the Cardinal would win.

Buckingham stopped suddenly and turned to d'Artagnan. "Five days!" he exclaimed. "That's all the time we will need."

Buckingham issued an immediate order: No ships were to be permitted to sail for France. That way, Milady wouldn't be able to get the diamonds to the Cardinal. No one questioned the Duke's order, for he was very powerful in the English government.

Next, the Duke called for his jeweler and showed him the ten diamond studs. He promised to pay the man well to make two more exactly like them. They must be finished within two days and be so perfect that no one would be able to tell the new from the old. The jeweler agreed and hurried away to begin working.

"We are not beaten yet, d'Artagnan!" exclaimed the Duke.

Two days later the new studs were ready. Buckingham and d'Artagnan examined them carefully. The jeweler had done well. It was impossible to tell that they weren't part of the original set. Now d'Artagnan could leave for France.

As his ship left Dover, d'Artagnan thought he saw Milady de Winter aboard one of the ships stranded in port. But his ship passed so quickly that he caught little more than a glimpse.

Back in France, d'Artagnan set off for Paris as fast as he could.

THE BALL

Everyone in Paris was talking about the ball. More than a week had been spent decorating the Hôtel de Ville with hundreds of candles and flowers of every color and variety.

The King arrived to the cheers of the crowd. Soon afterward the Queen entered the ballroom. She had never looked lovelier. But she was not wearing the diamonds. The Cardinal smiled triumphantly and quickly rushed over to tell King Louis.

The King strode to Queen Anne's side. "Madame," he demanded loudly, "why aren't you wearing the diamond studs when you knew it would give me such pleasure?"

The Queen saw Cardinal Richelieu watching

48

smugly from behind the King. "Sire," she told her husband, "I was afraid they would come to harm in such a large crowd. But I will do as you ask and send for them."

While the Queen and her ladies waited in another room, the Cardinal handed the King a box containing the two studs Milady de Winter had stolen from Buckingham.

"Ask the Queen where these come from," he suggested slyly.

But his triumph turned to rage when the Queen returned wearing all twelve diamonds.

"What does this mean?" asked the King, pointing to the studs the Cardinal had given him.

The Cardinal thought quickly. "I wished her Majesty to have them as a present," he said. "Not daring to offer them myself, I adopted this plan."

"I thank you kindly, your Eminence," said the Queen. But her smile showed that she understood the Cardinal's plot completely. "I am sure that these

The Queen gave him a diamond ring

two jewels must have cost you as much as all the others cost the King."

From behind a curtain, d'Artagnan watched the Queen's victory over the Cardinal. Apart from the King, the Cardinal, and the Queen herself, he was the only one in the crowded ballroom who knew what had happened. And only he knew the whole story.

Later, the Queen sent for him. She gave him a diamond ring in thanks for all he had done.

D'Artagnan put the ring on his finger and returned to the ball, feeling proud and happy. He was in favor with the King and with Monsieur de Tréville, and he had helped his Queen when she needed it most. Best of all, he had gained the friendship of three brave men, Athos, Porthos, and Aramis. D'Artagnan knew that one day he, too, would be a Musketeer.

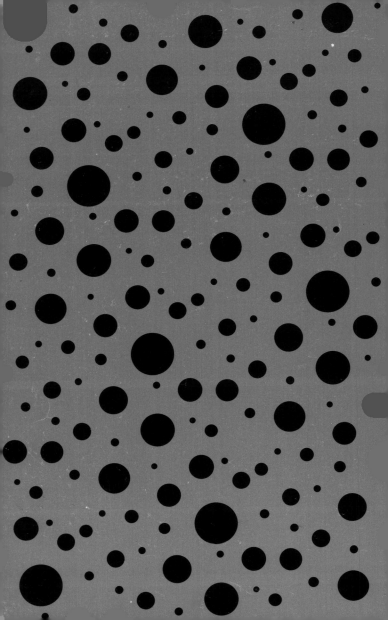